ALPHABET IN THE WILD!

Patrick O'Toole

DOVER PUBLICATIONS, INC.
Mineola, New York

For more Alphabetimals go to:
alphabetimals.com

Bibliographical Note
Alphabetimals—In the Wild! is a new work, first published by Dover Publications, Inc., in 2013. It is based on characters created by Patrick O'Toole on his website, alphabetimals.com

International Standard Book Number
ISBN-13: 978-0-486-49914-7
ISBN-10: 0-486-49914-6

Manufactured in the United States by Courier Corporation
49914601
www.doverpublications.com

NOTE

Welcome to the delightful world of Alphabetimals! This unique coloring book features some amazing creatures—ones that are part animal and part letters of the alphabet. So come and meet and color an array of adorable critters, from the Alligator A to the Zebra Z, and twenty-four in between! Plus, each alphabetimal is shown in its natural habitat, making coloring them even more fun.

7- A
1 C
1 D
1 E
1 I
5 J
2 K
1 M
1 N
1 S
1 W

Alligator

Bear

Cat

Elephant

Fish

Giraffe

Horse

Iguana

Jaguar

Kangaroo

Lion

Monkey

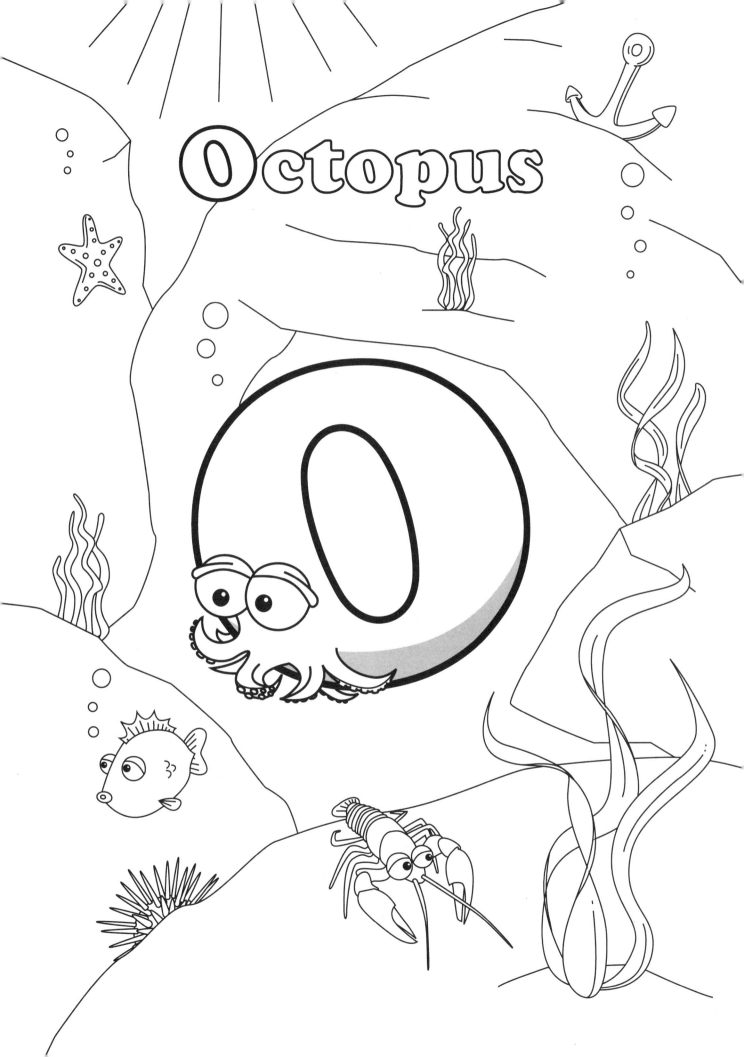

Platypus

Quail

Raccoon

Snake

Vulture

Worm

X-ray fish

Yak

Zebra